First published in English by Lantana Publishing Ltd in 2025.
Clavier House, 21 Fifth Road, Newbury RG14 6DN, United Kingdom
www.lantanapublishing.com | info@lantanapublishing.com

Originally published in Swedish as *Hemma hos Harald Henriksson*
by Lilla Piratförlaget, Sweden in 2018.

Text © Uje Brandelius, 2018
Illustration © Clara Dackenberg, 2018
English Translation © Nichola Smalley, 2025

The moral rights of the author, illustrator, and translator have been asserted.

All rights reserved. No part of this publication may be reproduced, stored in a retrieval system, or transmitted in any form or by any means, electronic, mechanical, photocopying, recording or otherwise, without the prior written permission of the copyright owner.

Distributed in the United States and Canada by Lerner Publishing Group, Inc.
241 First Avenue North, Minneapolis, MN 55401 U.S.A.
For reading levels and more information, look for this title at www.lernerbooks.com.
Cataloging-in-Publication Data Available.

Hardback ISBN: 978-1-83629-014-8
PDF ISBN: 978-1-83629-015-5
ePub3 ISBN: 978-1-83629-016-2

Printed and bound in China using sustainably sourced paper and plant-based inks.
Original artwork created using watercolor, gouache and paper cutouts.

The PLAYDATE

Uje Brandelius & Clara Dackenberg

Translated by Nichola Smalley

Today is going to be a great day. Me and Mom are going to Henry Henriksson's house.

I'm super excited to see Henry. He's so fun to play with and he has a funny dog.

I put some sandwiches in my backpack.

We leave our apartment. To get to Henry's house we have to take a bus then the subway then change to another line then a bus and then we have to walk for a while.

We walk past the toy shop with the robot in the window. I want that robot more than anything in the whole wide world but I know it costs so much money so I don't even ask.

When we get to Henry's house, Henry's mom opens the door. She says, come in, come in, make yourselves at home.

Me and Henry start playing straight away.

First we play chase with the dog. The dog's called Felix.

Then we play hide-and-seek. Henry's house is perfect.
There's millions and millions of rooms to hide in.

Then we play kings and servants.
I'm the king and Henry is my servant.
He has to bring me things and kiss
my boots.

Then we build a den.

Henry's mom says it's time to stop playing because Henry has to have lunch. He's having spaghetti bolognese.

Henry's mom asks if me and my mom want some too.

No, says Mom, there's no need. We brought sandwiches.

After lunch Henry wants to play computer games. I'm not very good at computers so I play with Felix instead.

Felix runs into a room I've never been in before.

There's an enormous bag full of toys. Right on the top there's a robot. It's exactly the same one I want more than anything in the whole wide world...

All of a sudden Henry's mom shouts, time for some fruit!

We eat some fruit. There's oranges, bananas, apples, pears, kiwis and some yellow things that aren't very nice. We can eat as much as we like! We watch Frozen on TV.

Then it's time to go home. We'll see you soon, says Henry's mom. I say, maybe Henry can come and play at our house some time. Hmm, maybe, says Henry's mom.

On the train I tell Mom that Henry is my best friend. I say how fun it was to play hide-and-seek and build a den and chase Felix.

But then I remember something. A really awful terrible thing. I go quiet. Then I start to cry. Mommy, I stole something! I get the robot out of my backpack.

Mom doesn't say anything at all.

When we get home Mom takes the robot and puts it up on the top shelf. I'll take it back to Henry's house next week, she says.

After dinner Mom watches TV. I tidy away my Lego and brush my teeth and put on my pajamas without Mom having to tell me to.

When Mom comes to tuck me in I ask her if she's mad at me. Mom looks at me for a really long time. Then she says, no, I'm not mad at you.

Sleep now, my love.